INSECTS ARE MY LIFE

story by Megan McDonald
pictures by Paul Brett Johnson

Orchard Books · New York

Text copyright © 1995 by Megan McDonald. Illustrations copyright © 1995 by Paul Brett Johnson.
All rights reserved. No part of this book may be reproduced or transmitted in any form or by any means,
electronic or mechanical, including photocopying, recording, or by any information storage or retrieval system,
without permission in writing from the Publisher.

Orchard Books, 95 Madison Avenue, New York, NY 10016

Manufactured in the United States of America. Printed by Barton Press, Inc.
Bound by Horowitz/Rae. Book design by Mina Greenstein.
The text of this book is set in 15 point Usherwood Medium. The illustrations are watercolor, colored pencil, and
pastel reproduced in full color.   10 9 8 7 6 5 4 3 2 1

Library of Congress Cataloging-in-Publication Data
McDonald, Megan. Insects are my life / story by Megan McDonald ; pictures by Paul Brett Johnson.   p.   cm.
"A Richard Jackson Book"—Half t.p.
Summary: No one at home or school understands Amanda Frankenstein's devotion to insects until
she meets Maggie.
ISBN 0-531-06874-9.   ISBN 0-531-08724-7 (lib. bdg.)
[1. Insects—Fiction. 2. Schools—Fiction. 3. Family life—Fiction.]   I. Johnson, Paul Brett, ill.
II. Title.   PZ7.M478419In   1995   [E]—dc20   94-21960

To Dick, for seeing

—M.M.

For Cheryl and Steve

—P.B.J.

The night that Andrew caught the fireflies in a jar, Amanda set them all free.

That was the first real clue that Amanda Frankenstein was crazy about insects. Bugs. Dozens of bugs. Cousins of bugs. Big bugs. Small bugs. Any bugs. All bugs. Creepy bugs. Crawly bugs. Slimy bugs. Climby bugs. Bugs with wings. Bugs that sing.

"How would *you* like to live in a peanut butter jar?" she asked her brother. "Bugs are people, too, you know!"

That night, she drew a giant dragonfly on the dinosaur poster in his room. And she slipped her ugliest rubber cockroach under his pillow before bed.

Amanda examined bugs. With her detective kit. Under rocks, hidden on leaves, in sidewalk cracks. She counted eleven different kinds in a single afternoon, including a seven-spotted ladybug.

Amanda collected bugs. Dead ones, of course. The skin of a grasshopper, the shell of a cicada, a perfect pair of dragonfly wings found after a thunderstorm. She collected bug cases. Once she hatched hundreds of tiny praying mantises right in her sock drawer. She collected mosquito bites. She counted twenty-two bites on one leg, and she was proud.

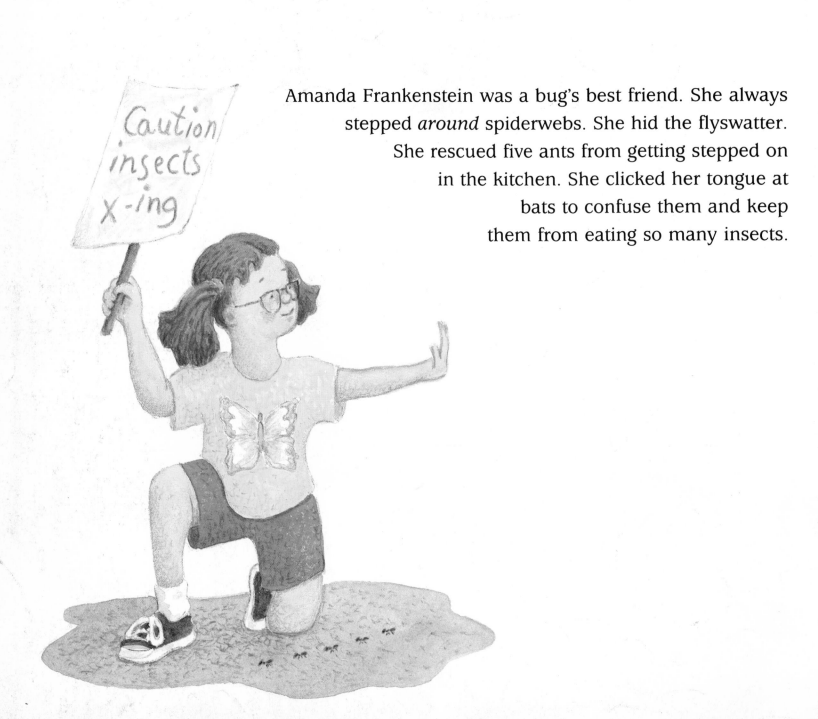

Amanda Frankenstein was a bug's best friend. She always stepped *around* spiderwebs. She hid the flyswatter. She rescued five ants from getting stepped on in the kitchen. She clicked her tongue at bats to confuse them and keep them from eating so many insects.

Amanda dreamed of hanging upside down on the ceiling like a fly. She imagined walking on water as nimbly as a water strider. Once she tried crawling forty miles on all fours, like an ant, and got as far as the backyard fence. "That's how far an ant could walk if it was a person!" she explained when her mother called her inside.

"Find something else to do until dinner, Amanda."

So Amanda watched her favorite movie, *The Fly,* two times in a row.

"My sister, the insect," said her brother. Amanda ignored him. Tonight, he would find her trick ice cube in his milk. The one with the dead fly in the center.

The End

After dark, Amanda opened her window wide and turned on the light so all the night bugs would fly in. She spied a yellow hawk moth, a garden tiger moth, and a lacewing fly. That is, until her mother found out. Thanks to Andrew.

"No bugs in the house, Amanda. When you're old enough to have your own house, you can have all the bugs you want there."

"When I'm all grown up, I'm going to be an entomologist," she told her mother, "and hatch rare butterflies in my living room."

"You can't be *that,*" said her brother.

"Then you can't be a dead bone digger either!"

"Paleontologist. They study dinosaurs. Dinosaurs are neat. Bugs are slimy."

"*Insects* are not slimy. Insects are fascinating. Insects are my life!"

On the first day of school, Amanda's mother begged her to wear her blue dress with the pink flowers. But Amanda insisted on wearing her ladybug T-shirt that said, AMANDA FRANKENSTEIN: FRIEND OF BUGS. She carried her new magnifying glass in a special pocket of her backpack. And she wore her purple dragonfly pin for good luck.

Ms. Scorpio, her teacher, had a dress the color of a luna moth and hair like a beehive. She led the class in a song,

"The ants go marching one by one, Hurrah! Hooray!
The last one stops to suck her thumb . . ."

and Amanda sang the loudest.

When it was time to choose an instrument to play, Amanda chose the triangle.

"You'll have to share with Victor," Ms. Scorpio told her. Victor had squinty little eyes like a slug and two spikes of hair that acted like antennae.

"Can you use those to smell?" Amanda asked.

"Bug off, Bug-eyes!" he hissed, pointing to her glasses.

The other kids laughed. "Four eyes! Four eyes!" they chanted. "Amanda has four eyes!"

"They're compound eyes," Amanda told them. "Like a wasp's." After that, Amanda played the tambourine. By herself.

The teacher took them on a bear hunt, over mountains, through forests. "I see . . . a cave. Can't go over it. Can't go around it. Have to go through it!" Amanda pretended with the others to look for a bear, but secretly she searched for an African killer beetle.

During circle time, Ms. Scorpio read *The Very Quiet Cricket*, and Amanda made the cricket sound, *"Cree! Cree! Cree!"* because the computer chip in the back of the book was broken. When it came her turn to recite a poem, Amanda made one up:

"Bugs are great
Bugs are good
Bugs live in your neighborhood."

That afternoon, Victor put a hairy spider on her seat. Amanda held it in her hand and pulled out her magnifying glass to study it. "A wolf spider!" she announced excitedly. "Did you know spiders are arthropods?"

"Amanda Frankenstein, you are a monster," Victor said.

"And you, Victor, are less than a flea. You are a stinkbug on the leaf of life."

"All right, that's enough. Time out for both of you."

Amanda had to sit in a chair and face the wall for ten minutes because of Victor. Tomorrow, Victor would find a Chinese water bug in his lunch box.

"I'm never going back to school," Amanda announced when she got home. She wrapped herself in a blanket and hid inside her cocoon. She tasted leaves and bark. She painted butterfly wings with eyespots like owls on them to scare away animals. And creeps like Victor. She tied the wings to her arms and flew down three steps. "First to fly!" she called.

"Amanda Frankenstein, get your feet off the table!" her mother scolded at dinner that night.

"But butterflies have taste buds on their feet," Amanda said.

"Well, please keep your taste buds on the floor," said her mother.

The next day was worse. When Amanda danced in circles like a bee, no other bees followed. When she pulled out her Mexican jumping beans for show-and-tell, no one believed there were caterpillars inside. And when Amanda pretended to have ears on her knees, like a cricket, the teacher told her to sit up straight and listen.

"Amanda Frankenstein thinks she's a bug!" yelled Victor. "A cricket! *Cree! Cree!*"

"Victor, you are a worm." Amanda told him.
"I thought you liked bugs."
"Worms are not insects, Victor."
"How do you know?"
"Because. Insects are my life!"
"Not again, you two. Amanda, come
sit over here by Maggie today."

"I like your glasses," whispered Amanda.
"They're for seeing underwater," Maggie said.
"Like whirligig beetles?" asked Amanda.

"Like crocodiles!" Maggie grinned widely, showing two pointy teeth. "Reptiles are my life!"